SNUFF
to the Rescue

BY ELISABETH BERESFORD

Illustrated by Gunvor Edwards

PUFFIN BOOKS/KESTREL

This is Snuffle.
He lives at No. 1.
He is just off for his
early morning walk.
He likes to make sure that everything is
all right on the street where he lives.
"It's better to be safe than sorry,"
Snuffle says.

3

First of all Snuffle went to see
    the new kitten at No. 3.
She was a very pretty, fluffy kitten
    called Kim.
She was playing on the street.
"You be careful," Snuffle said.
    "You might get run over.
    "Or you might get lost.
    "Or you might be STOLEN."
But Kim only chased her tail.

The next house is No. 5.
Ted and Tod live here.
They always say that they can do
       EVERYTHING better than Snuffle can.
Ted and Tod are always busy — and bossy.
"Morning Mr. Big Nose," they said.
And they went hurrying off.

A lot of puppies live at No. 7.
"Good morning puppies," said Snuffle.
"It's time for you to go to school.
Hurry up."
Out came all the puppies, barking and
jumping and chasing their tails.

The next house is No. 9.
Snuffle doesn't like this house.
It is a pet shop, and all the animals
   in it always look sad.
Mr. Beak lives here.
Mr. Beak is a very nasty man.
"Come along puppies," growled Snuffle.
   "Hurry up, hurry up."

Mr. Beak watched them from the
door of his shop.

8

At the crossing Snuffle made
all the puppies stop.
Then he waited for the cars to stop.
Suddenly Ted and Tod pushed past.
They ran across the road.
"Out of our way, Big Nose," they said.
"They've got no manners," growled Snuffle.
"Come along puppies, over you go."

Back at No. 3 Kim looked left
   and then right.
"Silly old Snuffle," she said.
   "I can look after myself.
   I shall go and play further down
   the street."

Off went Kim,
  but she got too close to the road.
A car roared past.
Kim couldn't move for a moment.
She was so frightened that
  her fur stood on end.

Suddenly a large hand came down
and picked up Kim.
"Silly little cat," said a gruff voice.
"You shouldn't be out alone.
I'll look after you."
And Kim was pushed into Mr. Beak's
deep dark pocket.

Snuffle came back from the park just
   as Mr. Beak went into his pet shop.
Outside No. 3
   Snuffle met Miss Tab and Mrs. Whiskers.
"Have you seen Kim?" they asked.
"She's not in the street
   and she's not in her house.
   Do you think you can find her, Snuffle?"

"Leave it to me," said Snuffle.
"I can follow all kinds of scent
    with my big nose!"
And off he went, sniff, sniff, SNIFF.

At the pet shop poor little Kim
was crying and shivering.
"What a pretty little kitten you are,"
said Mr. Beak.
"I will sell you for lots of money."
"I want to go home," mewed Kim.
"BE QUIET," said Mr. Beak.

He pushed her into a cage.

"Help, help," mewed Kim.

"Ssshh," said all the other animals.

   "If you make a noise Mr. Beak will be
   angry and he won't give us any food.
   PLEASE be quiet."

Snuffle was looking for Kim.
He searched Kim's house.
He searched from top to bottom.
All he found was the little red blanket
 on which she slept at night.
"I must think about this," said Snuffle.
 "I must think about this very carefully."

"Look at Snuffle trying to find that
     silly little kitten," said Tod and Ted.
     "Never mind, poor old Big Nose.
     You just have a rest
     while we find her!"
Snuffle didn't take any notice.
He just went sniff, sniff, SNIFF.

Then Snuffle got up and went
  slowly down the street.
He went past No. 5, and sniffed.
  Past No. 7, and sniffed.
When he came to No. 9 he stopped,
  and he went sniff, sniff, SNIFF.

Ted and Tod came bouncing by.
"What's all this?"
"What's happening?" asked Ted and Tod.
"Has that silly kitten got lost?
Never mind, we'll find her.
Out of our way old Big Nose."
And off they went.

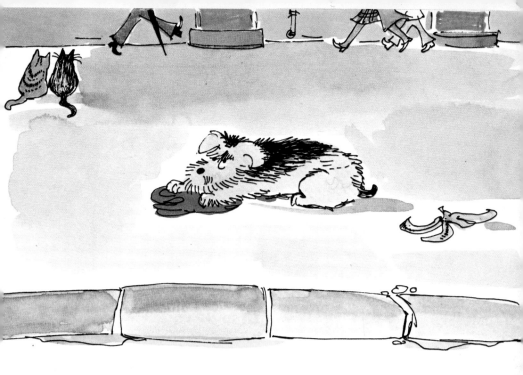

Snuffle sat and thought.
   And thought.
   And thought.
   AND THOUGHT.
   With his chin on the red blanket.
And then his nose twitched.

Then he went on to the crossing.
It was time for the puppies to come
back from school.

"Now then, puppies," said Snuffle.
"I've got a job for you.
You are all going to learn how
to follow a scent.
I want you to sniff this red blanket.
THEN I want you to try and find the
same scent in this street!"

DOGS
welcome
in this Park

Ted and Tod came bouncing up.
"Out of our way," they said.
    "We are busy finding that kitten."
And off they bounced.
Snuffle took no notice.
"Sniff away puppies," he said.
24

And they did.

And their noses took them past Mr. Beak,
and into the pet shop,
and right up to the cage where . . .
Kim was.

She WAS pleased to see the puppies.

So were all the other animals in
   the pet shop.
They barked and mewed and cried and
   yelped and shrieked and howled, and
   all jumped out of their cages.

"Get out, get out," shouted Mr. Beak.
"I can't stand the noise.
Get out all of you."

And they did.
All the animals ran, jumped, or flew back
to their old homes.

29

"Now remember," said Snuffle.
   "Don't ever go off like that again,
   you silly little kitten.
   Next time we might not be able
   to find you."
"Yes Snuffle," said Kim.
   "Thank you VERY much for rescuing me
   and rescuing all the other animals!"

30

Here's Snuffle again.
He's just off for his morning walk.
He wants to make sure that everything
    is all right.
Snuffle ALWAYS says,
    "It's better to be safe than sorry."

Kestrel Books, Penguin Books Ltd, Harmondsworth, Middlesex, England
Puffin Books, Penguin Books Ltd, Harmondsworth, Middlesex, England
Penguin Books Australia Ltd, Ringwood, Victoria, Australia
Penguin Books Canada Ltd, 41 Steelcase Road West, Markham, Ontario,
Canada
Penguin Books (NZ) Ltd, 182–190 Wairau Road, Auckland 10, New Zealand
Penguin Books Inc, 72 Fifth Avenue, New York, NY 10011, USA

Published simultaneously in Puffin Books and Kestrel Books 1975
ISBN Hardback 0 7226 5172 4
       Paperback 0 14 050.142 8
All rights reserved
Printed in Spain by Heraclio Fournier S.A.